Penny McKinlay grew up in Cheshire and read English
at Oxford University. She was inspired to write *Bumposaurus*
by her own daughter's vision problems. Penny is a television producer
and lives with her children in London. *Elephants Don't Do Ballet*, illustrated
by Graham Percy, was her first book for Frances Lincoln.

Britta Teckentrup has illustrated many
children's picture books and has worked on the BBC Teletubbies series.
Britta lives in Surrey with her family. Her previous titles
for Frances Lincoln are *Well, A Crocodile Can!* and *Babies Like Me!*,
both written by Malachy Doyle.

To Holly who helped, and to Scott – P.M.
To Vincent, our beautiful baby boy – B.T.

First published in Great Britain in 2003 by
Frances Lincoln Limited, 4 Torriano Mews, Torriano Avenue, London NW5 2RZ
www.franceslincoln.com

Distributed in the USA by Publishers Group West

First paperback edition published in Great Britain in 2004 and in the USA in 2006.

British Library Cataloguing in Publication Data available on request

ISBN 13: 978-1-84507-516-3
ISBN 10: 1-84507-516-1

The illustrations are collage and digital imaging.
Set in Jacoby and Bembo

Printed in Singapore

1 3 5 7 9 8 6 4 2

Bumposaurus

Penny McKinlay

Illustrated by **Britta Teckentrup**

FRANCES LINCOLN CHILDREN'S BOOKS

There was once a baby dinosaur who was so short-sighted he couldn't find his way out of his egg.

BUMP! BUMP!

BUMP!

he went inside the shell.

At last his mother heard him bumping and helped him out. "I think we'll call you Bumposaurus!" she said.

Bumposaurus ran off straight past his brothers and sisters.
He ran over the edge of the sandy hollow,
he fell down a very steep hill,

and he landed in a very **deep**

bog.

"Mother!"

called the other baby dinosaurs.
"Bumpy's stuck!"

Mother hauled him out, licking the mud lovingly
off his nose.

"He's obviously the adventurous type!" she said to Father.

"Come and play chase, Bumpy!" cried his brothers and sisters. "You're IT!" And they ran off giggling.

Bumposaurus **s t r e t c h e d** his long neck this way and that.

"Where are you?" he called.

"We're over here!" they cried, creeping closer.
Still he couldn't see them.

"Here!" they cried, creeping closer still.

"Oh, there you are!" cried Bumposaurus.
He swung suddenly round and knocked
them down like skittles.

BUMP!

BUMP!

BUMP!

Mother gave them each a loving lick.
"Lunch-time!" she said.

Lunch was leaves. Lunch was always leaves.
"Not leaves again," moaned the babies.
"Now children," scolded their father.
"You know we Brontosauruses don't believe
in eating other dinosaurs!"

Bumposaurus began to munch obediently
on what lay before him.

It turned out to be his sister's tail.

"Father!" she shrieked. "Bumpy's eating me!"
"Bumposaurus!" said Father sternly.
"Eating dinosaurs is wrong!"

After lunch, Bumposaurus
went off to explore.

Bump!

His head met something hard.
He looked up. The something
stretched high above him.

"Sorry, Father," he said. "I didn't see you."

Father said nothing.

"I know you're cross about me eating Bella. I didn't mean to."

Still Father said nothing.

"You see, Father, I think there's something wrong with me. I feel as though I'm different from the others."

And he poured out the whole story.

But Father still
said nothing.
He couldn't,
because in fact
he was a
tree.

"Oh well," sighed Bumposaurus. "If you're that angry, I'll have to leave home."
   And he set off.

Bumposaurus came to the edge of a wide river. "Lucky these logs are here. I don't have to get my feet wet."

"Funny... there doesn't seem
to be anybody else about!"

By now Bumposaurus felt like
giving up and going home.
He was covered in bumps.
He was tired and lonely and
longing for a loving lick from Mother.
At last he stumbled into a sandy hollow.

"Home!"

he cried in joy.

And he snuggled up cosily
and fell asleep. . .

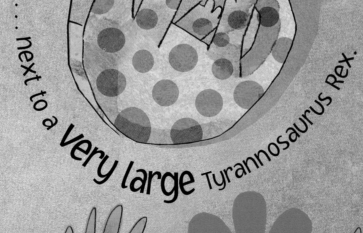

. . . next to a **very large** Tyrannosaurus Rex.

The Tyrannosaurus was sleeping off a heavy meal, most definitely not of leaves! He was very surprised when he woke to find a small Brontosaurus fast asleep in his nest.

"Yum!" he said, and gave Bumpy an experimental lick.

"You're not my mother," yelped Bumpy, waking up with a jump.

"No, but you're my **pudding!"**

And the Tyrannosaurus grinned
a horrible grin, bristling with
razor-sharp teeth.

But just at that moment there came the thunderous sound of forty galloping feet. Ten furious Brontosaurus faces glared down into the hollow.

"put my son down!"

bellowed Father.

"Eating dinosaurs is wrong!"

"Quite right, Quite right!"
the Tyrannosaurus said quickly.
"What was I thinking of?
Please excuse me!"
And he ran off.

When Bumposaurus got home, his mother gave him the most loving lick ever. "Say hello to Grandma, Bumposaurus," she said.

"Where?"

said Bumposaurus

"Here," said a gentle voice, and a soft and wrinkled face
bent close to his. "Now you can see me, can't you?" she said.
"What are those circles round your eyes, Grandma?"
asked Bumpy.
"Try them on, and see, little one," she said.

Bumposaurus slid the glasses on to his nose. At once, a wonderful world of **smiling** faces leapt out at him.

At last he could see!

More Titles from Frances Lincoln Children's Books

Flabby Tabby

Penny McKinlay

Illustrated by Britta Teckentrup

Tabby's life is not exactly an endless round of activity – but when
a kitten arrives, everything changes. The kitten is always bouncing
in HER basket and eating HER breakfast, so Tabby hatches
a secret feline fitness plan to show Fit Kit what's what!

ISBN 1-84507-090-9

Elephants Don't Do Ballet

Penny McKinlay

Illustrated by Graham Percy

When Esmeralda the elephant wants to be a ballerina,
Mummy's not so sure – after all, elephants don't do ballet.
But Esmeralda always gets what she wants.

ISBN 1-84507-187-5 (US)
ISBN 0-7112-1130-2 (UK)

Fancy That!

Gillian Lobel

Illustrated by Adrienne Geoghegan

There is a nest of white eggs in the hot sand,
almost ready to hatch. But whose eggs are they?
Will the animals guess what kind of babies are inside
before the eggs begin to crack...

ISBN 1-84507-335-5

Frances Lincoln titles are available from all good bookshops.
You can also buy books and find out more about your favourite titles,
authors and illustrators on our website: www.franceslincoln.com